For Grandma and Grandpa
—J.S.

To Lauren, Madeline, Nora, Hazel, Nina, Annika,
Jack, Oliver, and Eloise. Friends forever.
—J.K.

Balzer + Bray is an imprint of HarperCollins Publishers.

The Night Is for Darkness
Text copyright © 2020 by Jonathan Stutzman
Illustrations copyright © 2020 by Joseph Kuefler
All rights reserved. Manufactured in China.
No part of this book may be used or reproduced in any manner whatsoever without written permission except
in the case of brief quotations embodied in critical articles and reviews. For information address HarperCollins
Children's Books, a division of HarperCollins Publishers, 195 Broadway, New York, NY 10007.
www.harpercollinschildrens.com

ISBN 978-0-06-291253-4

Typography by Dana Fritts
20 21 22 23 24 SCP 10 9 8 7 6 5 4 3 2 1
❖
First Edition

NIGHT
IS FOR
DARKNESS

Written by
Jonathan Stutzman

Illustrated by
Joseph Kuefler

BALZER + BRAY
An Imprint of HarperCollinsPublishers

The night is for darkness
and bright golden beams.

For discovering eyes
are not what they seem.

The night is for running
barefoot and fast,

through sweet meadow flowers
and tall dewy grass.

The night is for hiding.
And searching
and finding.

For spooky tall forests.
For paths long and
winding.

The night is for lightning.
The night is for glowing.

The night is for planning,
for packing
and going.

The night is for darkness
and all that it brings,

the shadows and flickers
and creatures with wings.

The night is for foxes
and wise-looking owls.

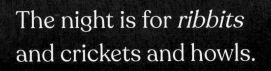

The night is for *ribbits*
and crickets and howls.

The night is for searching
for worlds not your own.

The night is for finding
the love in your home.

The night is for stories,
for reading
and telling.

Of magic and strangers,
and beans
they are selling.

The night is for secrets,
for prayers
and whispers.

By mothers and fathers,
by brothers and sisters.

The night is for holding.
The night is for kisses.
Hushed lullaby songs
and falling-star wishes.

our new
home

The night is for darkness
and soft silver beams,
for closing your eyes
and entering dreams.

*The night is for darkness
and soft silver beams,
for closing your eyes
and entering dreams.*